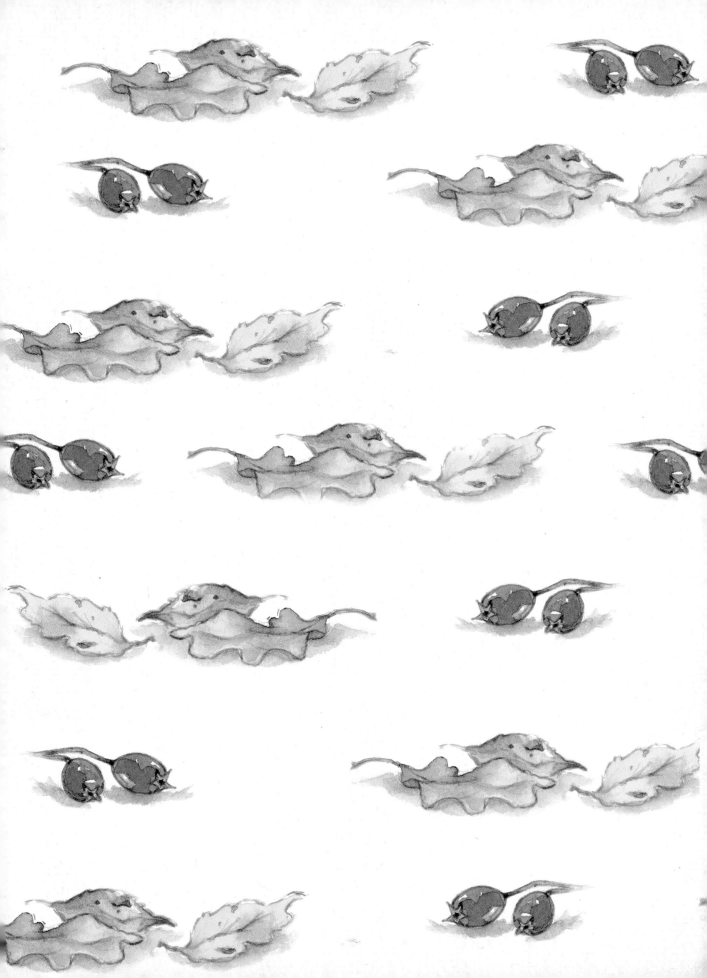

For Trudi – a friend dearly missed L.G.
To my dear friend Julie – many thanks G.H.

First published in Great Britain in 2007
by Piccadilly Press Ltd,
5 Castle Road, London NW1 8PR
www.piccadillypress.co.uk

Text copyright © Lynne Garner, 2007
Illustrations copyright © Gaby Hansen, 2007

Designed by Simon Davis
Printed and bound in China
Colour reproduction by Dot Gradations

ISBN: 978 1 85340 844 1 (hardback)
ISBN: 978 1 85340 849 6 (paperback)

3 5 7 9 10 8 6 4 2

A catalogue record of this book is available from the British Library

A Book for Bramble

Lynne Garner
Illustrated by Gaby Hansen

Piccadilly Press • London

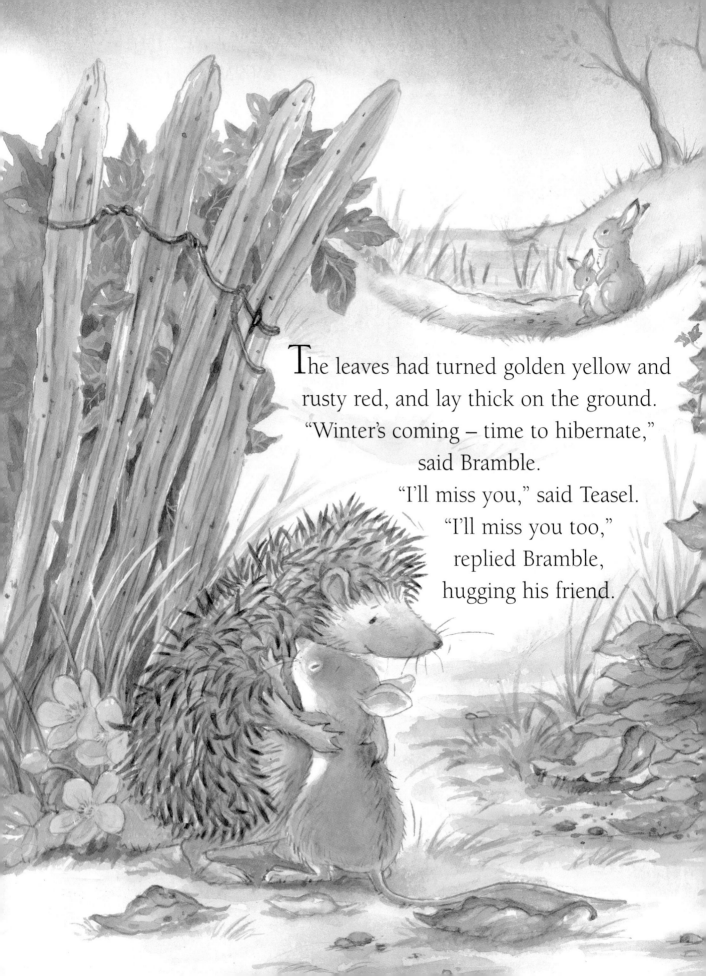

The leaves had turned golden yellow and
rusty red, and lay thick on the ground.
"Winter's coming – time to hibernate,"
said Bramble.
"I'll miss you," said Teasel.
"I'll miss you too,"
replied Bramble,
hugging his friend.

Teasel watched as Bramble and the rest of
his family crept to their nest under the
upside-down wheelbarrow.

At suppertime that evening Teasel rolled his roasted hazelnuts and chestnuts around his plate.

"You're missing Bramble, aren't you?" asked his mother.

Teasel nodded sadly.

After supper, Teasel was bored.

"Why don't you draw a picture?"
suggested his mother.

"I know, I'll draw one for
Bramble!" said Teasel.
"And I'll write to him,
too, telling him all
about winter. I'll make
a book for Bramble."

Teasel fetched his pencils and a large
sketch book and sat by the roaring fire.

Teasel wrote A BOOK FOR BRAMBLE
in big letters, and began.

Dear Bramble, I'm going to tell
you what's happening while
you're asleep. Then we can share
winter when you wake up.

and i will write
very day.

Teasel drew a picture of the upside-down
wheelbarrow where Bramble was now sleeping.
When he had finished, he closed the book
and hid it under his pillow.

The days rolled by and
Teasel still missed his
friend. At the winter
feast there were lots of
delicious things: nuts,
pumpkin pie, and warm
blackcurrant squash.

"If only Bramble was
here," thought Teasel.

Teasel sat by the pond, hoping the noise of the party would wake his friend. As he dipped his tail into the cold water and watched the ripples, Mrs Squirrel came over.

"Teasel, come and join in the games."
"But I want Bramble to be here. He's my BEST friend," said Teasel.
"I know, dear, but you can share the fun with him in your book."

Teasel was very tired after the party,
but he had lots to write in
Bramble's book that day.

We made a bonfire.
The flames were
red and yellow and
warmed our
cold noses.

Mrs Squirrel hid
nuts, which we had to
find. It was so much fun.
I wish you'd been there!

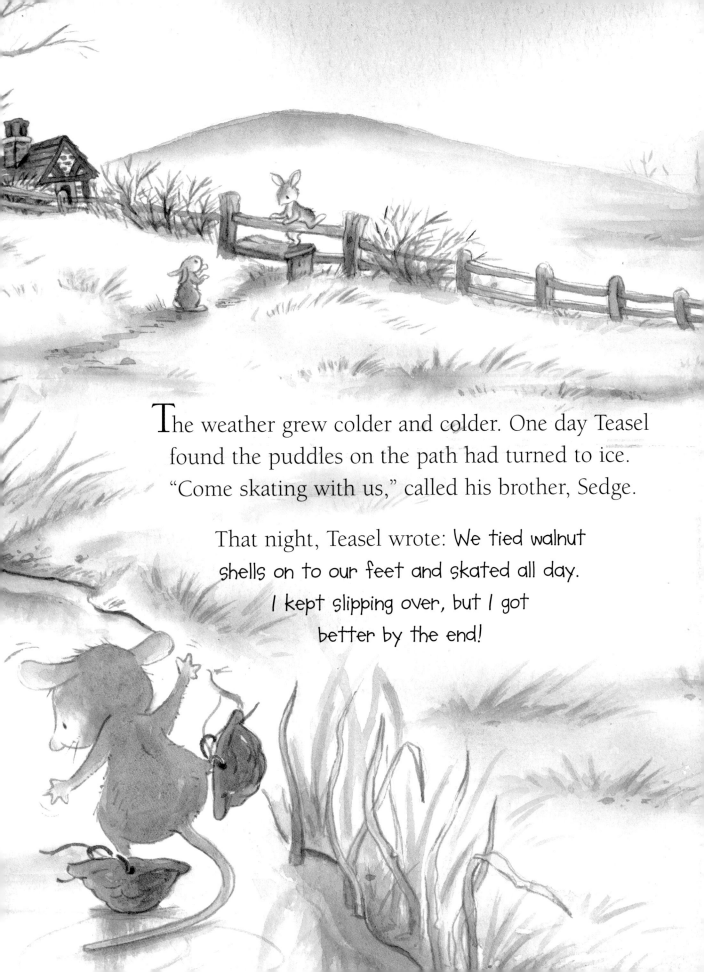

The weather grew colder and colder. One day Teasel
found the puddles on the path had turned to ice.
"Come skating with us," called his brother, Sedge.

That night, Teasel wrote: We tied walnut
shells on to our feet and skated all day.
I kept slipping over, but I got
better by the end!

The days became colder still. When Teasel looked out of the window one morning, everything seemed to be covered in a thick white blanket.

"It's snowing! It's snowing!" he shouted, running into the kitchen.

"We know," said his sister, Meadow. "We're going to play in the snow after breakfast!"

"Bramble would love this," said Teasel as he gathered another pawful of snow. "I do miss him."

"I know. Let's make a snow-hedgehog in his honour," said Sedge.

That night, Teasel drew a picture of the
snow-hedgehog for Bramble, and wrote:
It was huge. I wish you could have seen it.
When we finished, we had a snowball fight.
Then Sedge broke off some icicles
and we had ice lollies.

Teasel was having lots of fun that winter –
but still he missed Bramble.

Gradually, spring came.
Flowers poked through the
earth, and the sun grew stronger.
Teasel knew that Bramble
would soon wake up, and he took
a basket of nuts with him when
he went to the wheelbarrow.
Bramble would be hungry
after his long sleep.

Then at last Teasel heard shuffling coming from the wheelbarrow.
One by one, Bramble's family crept out
into the sunlight.

Finally Bramble emerged,
yawning and stretching.
"Bramble," Teasel shouted,
running to greet his friend.
"I MISSED you!"

"I missed you too!" said Bramble. "I know I did because I dreamed about you."

"I made a book for you, so that we could share winter," said Teasel. "Do you want to see it?"

"Oh yes! I've always wanted to know what winter was like!" said Bramble.

And the two friends sat by
the pond together as
Bramble began to read,
"Dear Bramble . . ."